For Nathan and Francesca

A TEMPLAR BOOK

Devised and produced by
The Templar Company plc
Pippbrook Mill, London Road,
Dorking, Surrey RH4 1JE, England

ISBN 1-898784-36-1

Printed and bound in Italy

The

GOLDEN PEAR

Written and illustrated by
Helen Ward

TEMPLAR

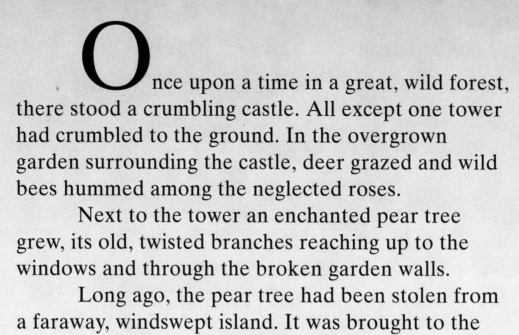

Once upon a time in a great, wild forest, there stood a crumbling castle. All except one tower had crumbled to the ground. In the overgrown garden surrounding the castle, deer grazed and wild bees hummed among the neglected roses.

Next to the tower an enchanted pear tree grew, its old, twisted branches reaching up to the windows and through the broken garden walls.

Long ago, the pear tree had been stolen from a faraway, windswept island. It was brought to the magnificent castle with great ceremony and carefully planted among the neatly clipped hedges behind the high castle walls.

Only a few knew one secret of the stolen tree—its fruit was made of *gold*.

Kings were born and aged and died while waiting for the pear tree to flower. Wars were fought and won and lost, but not a fruit appeared.

No one knew the deepest secret of the pear tree—its magic would never allow a pear to fall in the castle garden. The ancient enchantment, as deep as the tree's twisting roots, bound each golden fruit to the island where the magical pears first grew. Captive in the garden, the enchanted tree could not produce a single golden pear.

The castle slowly grew older and its cracks grew larger. In time, the tree was forgotten, and the garden and the castle were forgotten too . . . forgotten by everyone except a lonely, wandering wizard.

Driven away from home after home, the magician's careless spells and experiments had once kept whole towns awake and set villages on fire. No one wanted him for a neighbor, and he soon forgot how it felt to be wanted and loved. He grew afraid of people and tried to avoid them. When he found the abandoned castle, he claimed it for his home.

Alone here in the center of the forest, he could send huge, colorful sparks into the sky until they singed the moon. He could make slate-rattling explosions and there was no one to complain.

The wizard's lonely life passed as the wilderness crept over the borders of the garden. Weeds and wildflowers grew by the strong, gnarled trunk of the old pear tree. Squirrels and birds built untidy nests among its thick branches.

One year, the pear tree's leaves grew larger and glossier than ever before. Even the wizard began to notice the curious tree.

All through that winter, the wizard searched deep in the castle's library. He measured maps and

watched the stars. When his complicated calculations were complete, he settled down to wait patiently for the tree to bear its golden fruit.

The wizard watched from his window through the summer when the forest all around was green and butterflies landed on his nose.

He watched from his window through the autumn when the green turned to gold and the owls roosted on his shoulders.

He watched through the winter when the forest became an icy snowscape and mice nested in his hair.

In the spring, a tiny, white blossom opened at the top of the tree and a long-forgotten smile pulled at the corners of the wizard's mouth.

The petals fell and, slowly through the summer, a small, green pear began to grow.

The pear turned a richer yellow each day and then ripened from yellow to gold. It shone in the bright sunshine and gleamed in the light of the moon.

The wizard watched and waited for the golden pear to fall. But other eyes were caught by its gleam, and one pair of eyes belonged to a greedy crow.

In the brightness of the first frosty morning, the wizard yawned and blinked, and in that blink down swooped the crow. It took the golden pear by the stem in its broad, gray beak, flapped its wings, and took off like an old umbrella into the clear, blue sky.

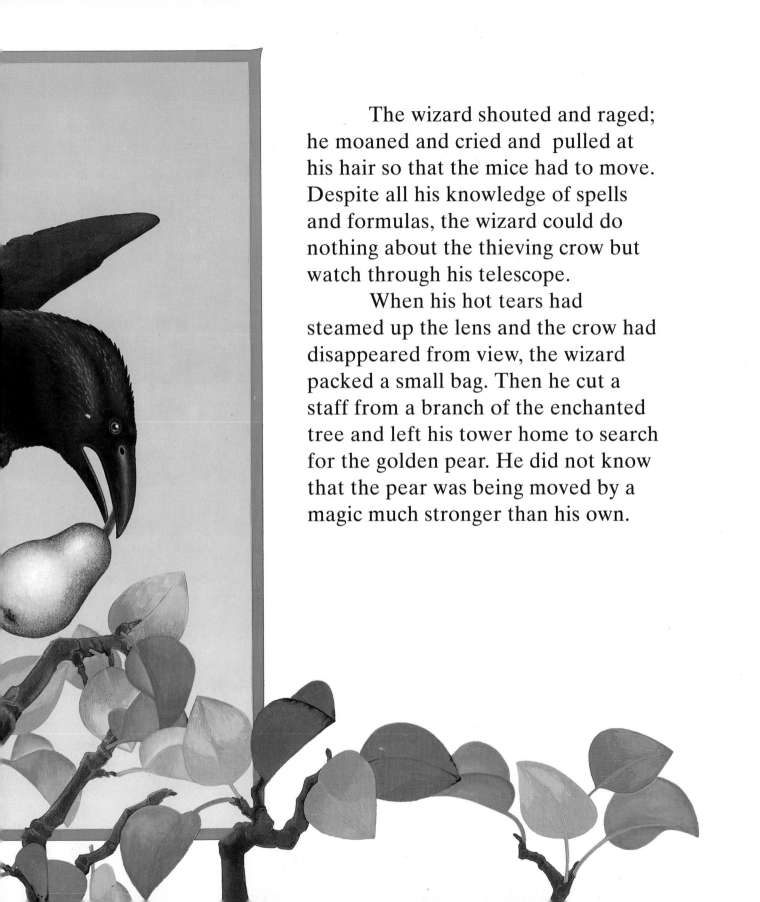

The wizard shouted and raged; he moaned and cried and pulled at his hair so that the mice had to move. Despite all his knowledge of spells and formulas, the wizard could do nothing about the thieving crow but watch through his telescope.

When his hot tears had steamed up the lens and the crow had disappeared from view, the wizard packed a small bag. Then he cut a staff from a branch of the enchanted tree and left his tower home to search for the golden pear. He did not know that the pear was being moved by a magic much stronger than his own.

The crow flew on through the chilly morning sky over the forest. Soon he was joined by another.

"What's that you've got there?" he croaked. But the first crow would not answer for fear of dropping his prize.

The two crows flew on, but curiosity brought a third.

"What's that he's got there?" the third crow cawed to the second.

"I don't know," answered the second, and he asked the first crow again. Still the crow would not reply, and all three flew on . . .

A fourth then joined the group, and he asked the third who asked the second who asked the first who was still flying on . . .

"What's that you've got there?"

The first crow was infuriated with their infernal questioning.

"It's a p . . . ," he squawked, and the pear fell out of his open beak and through the sky.

With a flurry of feathers and a knocking of heads, a scramble of beaks and a clashing of claws, all four crows tumbled after it, squawking and cackling. But the pear disappeared through the roof of the forest below.

It crashed through the leaves and the thin twigs. It bounced off the branches and landed with a thump on the forest floor. It rolled and turned, over and over, until it splashed with a silvery shower into a stream.

The pear bobbed with the current, gently twisting and turning its way downstream.

Three otters were hunting for their breakfast when the first and oldest patted the pear with a paw.

"Well, this isn't a fish," she said as the little group swam in and out of the patchy sunlight.

"And it isn't an eel," said the second and middle-est as they paddled around the knots of green water weed.

"And it certainly isn't breakfast," said the third and youngest.

In three rippling dives, the otters were gone, leaving the pear to drift on.

The stream joined other streams and formed a river. It flowed through woodlands and thickets and became wider. It passed through fields and marshes and became wider still. It rolled into a great, sandy estuary that fed the sea, and into the tide went the golden pear. In the wide ocean, the pear was curled into waves and pulled into currents—tossed from stormy, white crest to crest.

Beneath the waves a small fish looked hungrily at the pear. A medium-sized fish looked hungrily at the small fish, and a big fish looked at them both, wondering how they would taste.

Snap! The small fish swallowed the pear.

Gulp!! The medium-sized fish swallowed the small fish.

CRUNCH!!! The big fish swallowed them all!

He had barely enough time to enjoy his meal when a delicious-looking piece of maggoty ship biscuit drifted by. The big fish took a greedy bite. Just too late, he felt a hook. He was caught on a fisherman's line . . .

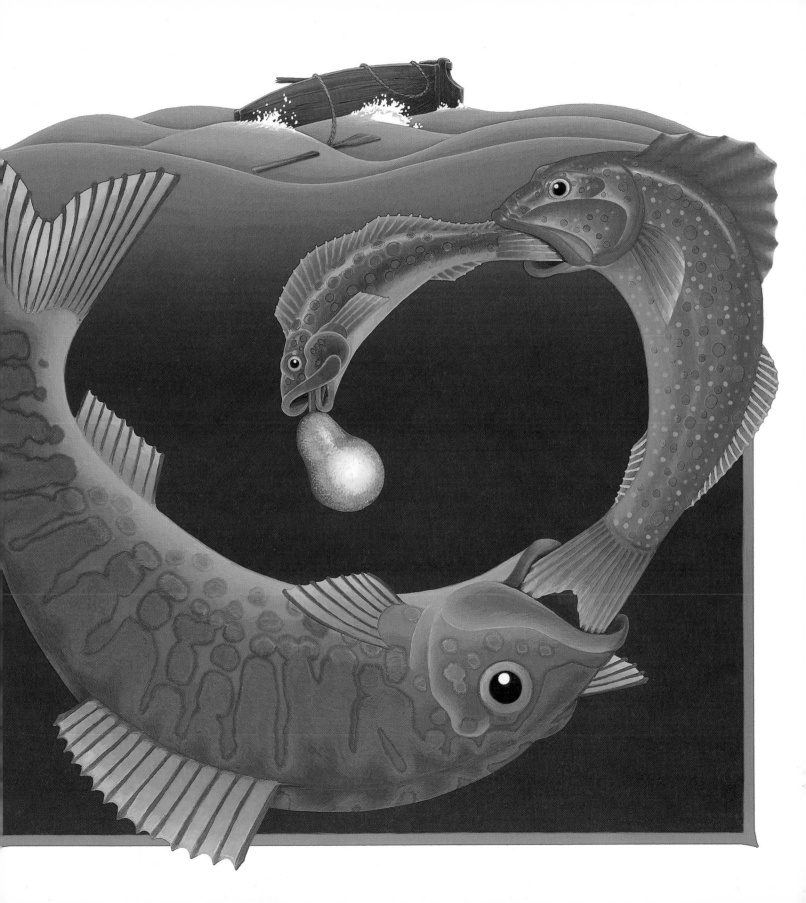

On stormy seas, a little boat pitched high and low. The mast was gone and the oars had been snatched and broken by the waves. The boat leaked like a sieve and carried a sailor who was lost at sea.

Having caught and eaten a fish, he now lay asleep. Held in his hands was a pear, dirty but smooth as a pebble.

The sailor dreamed of a rescue ship and of strong winds taking him home. He dreamed of the land and of a wild, green forest.

The pear slipped from his fingers and rolled into the bottom of the boat. The seed inside the fruit sent out its roots. They wrapped around the boat, knitting and knotting together its weakening planks.

A slim stem grew toward the sky, as tall and
straight as a mast. A crown of branches, twigs, and
leaves spread from its growing trunk.

When the sailor awoke in the comforting
shade of the rustling leaves, he thought his dreams
had come true.

Though the boat was still rocked by the waves, each leaf caught the wind like a small sail.

On the endless horizon, there appeared in the distance a small patch of cloud. Soon, a dark island could be seen beneath the mists and the wheeling specks of seabirds.

By the evening, the little boat had grounded on a warm, shimmering black beach. The sailor pulled the pear tree boat out of the reach of the sea, and then he slept on the sand nearby.

During the night, the tree splintered the planks of the little boat. By morning, it was rooted deep and fast in the soft sand, home at last.

The next day, the sailor explored his new home. He drank from a stream of fresh, clear water which ran out across the beach. He built a warm fire from the driftwood scattered over the rocks. He watched seabirds tending their nests and turtles plowing their way up and down the dark shoreline.

Far away in another land, the wizard still searched for the stolen pear. He had walked for weeks and miles, and miles and weeks over windswept moors and through distant fields. At night, he had quietly passed by farms and villages.

He plodded along backroads to avoid people, and in all this time he spoke to nobody. He did not dare to set off a single spark to light a lonely fire.

Each day's walk wore his pear tree staff down so much that at night he had to plant it in the ground so it could grow again.

Not a single spell or formula could help him. In all his searching, he found not one sign of the golden pear.

The wizard's beard had grown to tickle his bare toes and the pear tree staff had renewed itself completely many times when, finally, the land ran out. There was only the sea before him.

He sat on the edge of the cliff feeling miserable. He sighed like the wind in a wave and shed salty tears.

Far below some fishermen were pulling crab pots into their boat. The wizard watched idly as the boat rolled on the sea. Suddenly, he noticed its name—*The Golden Pear*! He was so surprised that he jumped to his feet and fell off the cliff into the sea, frightening the seabirds as he passed.

The kindly fishermen pulled the wizard out of the water. He was the heaviest, most useless, and most worried-looking catch they had ever pulled aboard. He sat with the broken pots, the crabs, and the lobsters until the day's work was done. Then the fishermen took the wizard back home with them.

The wizard sat in front of their fire, steaming enough to peel the wallpaper. Gradually, as he warmed his toes, his fear of people began to fade. The fishermen were so kind to him that, eventually, he summoned the courage to ask why their boat had been named *The Golden Pear*.

The older fisherman began the story . . . many years ago, his great grandfather had been caught in a storm at sea. Lost and adrift in the ocean, he had been saved by a pear tree mast and a sail of leaves. He had landed and lived on a faraway island for three years. Each year, the tree that had saved him produced a golden pear. At last, a passing ship had brought him home.

The old man fetched down a small, wooden box from a high shelf. He carefully opened the lid to reveal three golden pears wrapped in yellowing newspaper and gleaming in the firelight. Each one of them was as beautiful as the single pear the crow had stolen so many years before.

The wizard and the fishermen talked long into the night. They searched out charts and logbooks. They calculated and counted, navigating the seas in their imaginations.

In the dark, early hours of the next day, the wizard nodded into uneasy dreams of deep, rolling oceans and dark, volcanic islands—still searching for the golden pear. When he awoke, he knew he must finish the years of lonely searching by seeing the pear tree for himself. He knew he must leave the comfort of the little fishing village.

As the sun came up, the wizard packed his small bag and said good-bye to his only friends. The fishermen gave the wizard a tiny boat, and he gave them his pear tree staff. It was time to go.

Never had he felt quite so lonely as when he sailed his tiny boat over the vast sea in search of a far horizon.

For days and weeks he sailed through storms and gales. He ate maggoty ship biscuits and chewed raw fish. He ate his boots and chewed his beard. He drank raindrops collected in his hat.

At last, one pleasant, breezy dawn, he saw white clouds on the horizon. By noon, the shape of an island was clear. By sunset, he could see the island, not barren and dark as he had imagined—but rounded and green, with the foliage and branches of countless pear trees. Glinting and gleaming in the last rays of sunlight were the golden pears, like lanterns among the leaves.

The wizard sailed into a cove and pulled up his boat onto the darkening shore. He sat on the sand gazing at the wild forest of trees that had grown from just one golden pear. He knew that he would stay.

One day, he stared at the sea, deeply missing
the small fishing village and remembering the good
friends he had longed for and then left behind.

The wind rattled the autumn leaves like fiery
flags and whistled through the grass. It lifted the
white waves toward the sky—and brought sails over
the horizon!

A bright, new boat, almost a ship, sailed toward the island. The fishermen were coming!

They brought their families with them, and their children planted those three golden pears from long ago at the edge of the pear tree forest.

A small, new harbor began to grow beneath the shining woods. The old wizard was happier than he had ever been before.

Once a year, when the moon, as round as a plate, shone a path across the sea, he would rework his noisy, old experiments to the delighted joy of the islanders.

Bright, dazzling sparks exploded into the starry sky, flying high above the black peak to fall in flickering showers and twisting spirals.

The sparkling lights reflected in the faces of the old wizard and his many friends, glimmered in the forest of shining autumn leaves, and gleamed among the golden pears.